ALICE IN G
And Othe

Maya Hornick

Copyright © 2022 by Maya Hornick

Chapter 1 – Red Fox at Dawn

The sun disappears behind a cloud. I reach for my jumper. The chill breeze takes the warmth from my body and the sky has a greyish, shadowy cast. I suck in the air, cool and refreshing before the sun radiates down again its penetrating heat and I head for the shade of the apple tree in the corner of the allotment. I planted an apple pip thirty years ago and now I have this, the tree that shades me and provides worm-eaten fruit for the sweet pies I make from my grandmother's recipe.

The foxes love this part of the allotment too. I relax in my chair when over the fence leaps an agile reddish-brown form with a fluffy, white-tipped tail. It crouches low, surveying the area before scampering off in search of something that I can't provide. It looks back once and locks its eyes to mine with suspicion, with a warning. I'm glad it hasn't pounced on me yet, though it once attacked one of the lace-up boots that I left in a corner by the shed, dragging it across the allotment while I was unaware, and biting off the shoelaces.

I think the foxes and I have tacitly agreed an uneasy truce. Apart from the ravaged shoe incident, we don't bother each other. My allotment is merely a passing-through point onto somewhere more interesting. I wonder where. I like the surprise of seeing the flash of amber fur and gleaming black eyes before the fox disappears from view. The appearance of one is like a warning to be vigilant, to be prepared for the unexpected. In this world, anything might happen, and as my father would say, "... and it probably will".

Back in the day, I used to visit here with my grandmother and sunbathe on the deckchairs between the greenhouse and the shed; a little secluded spot she decorated with Japanese pink pebbles to look like a

Zen garden. All that's needed is some grey gravel to rake and it would be perfect; a place to meditate away from the throng of the city.

At the top of the allotments is a busy main road where the sound of traffic zooming past used to bother me. That was until gran said to think of the sound of the passing vehicles as that of a gushing waterfall. Now I do just that.

I am growing edible flowers this year, so I can eat like the Elizabethans did, save for the pheasant. I'll have them with a vegetarian nut roast instead with chutney and gravy to boot. All the trimmings, as they say. No holding back. When it comes to food, I try and use it medicinally, as my grandmother did. She died at 103 and was bright as a button until the end, so she must have been on the right track, though I think that secretly she wanted to be immortal, like the figures from Chinese mythology.

By all the trimmings, I mean with sweet purple potatoes and seaweed, much like the Okinawans eat. They are a very long-living group of people. But not only do they have a beautiful environment in which to dwell in a place surrounded by nature and the sea, but they have each other too. Social connections are what keep the mind strong and healthy. It prevents us from going mad with dementia, so it is said. It all depends on the company one keeps, I would have thought. Some folks can drive you around the twist if you're not careful.

Take my half-sister, for example. She likes to tell me every little thing that's on her mind, precisely because she knows it annoys me, or so it would seem. The detail she goes into is a thing of wonder and to some, even fascinating. But to me it gets tedious. I like to keep things simple, to keep track of everything necessary to live a good life, and nothing more.

I retired six years ago due to workplace stress. Teaching teenagers embroidery wouldn't pose too much of a hassle, one would have thought, but that wasn't the case at all. Something about needlework made the children tetchy. Instead of a calm and relaxed atmosphere, there was tension and the frequent outbreak of squabbles over petty things.

Several of them became very grumpy and rude towards me when I tried to help them grasp the finer points of crocheting a simple cushion-cover. When the head-teacher found some marijuana joints being passed around the sixth form common room one lunch break, I knew that teaching them crochet had been a step too far. It can bamboozle the cleverest of people at the best of times. It was then that I realised this school was more St. Trinian's than Enid Blyton's Malory Towers.

I leave food out for the fox sometimes. Today it's a raw egg and some berries. These berries are from the supermarket and not from the allotment – that crop has been eaten by the birds. I feel like such a terrible misfit at times, from some long-lost bygone era, where people would visit for afternoon tea sipped out of delicate bone china teacups, and admire the view onto a manicured lawn as we sit in the shade eating lemon sponge cake. It's 1993 and things are different these days.

Now I'm into experimental cooking. Whatever is available, I can bake a cake out of it, even if it is mushrooms and bananas. I like to see which weird flavours go together. Like with people, unexpected combinations can sometimes work. Take Alice and me. She is a bereaved mother I met at the library one rainy afternoon, the drizzle dripping down the windowpanes in wiggly patterns. I had been absently staring out onto the library garden for too long. Alice wanted a book from a shelf she couldn't reach so asked me if I could get it for her, being a good foot taller than her. I said of course, and then a conversation began about the embroidery book I was in the middle of reading.

Alice left school at sixteen to look after her baby boy. I have never had any children. She is very brave, braver than me. She has a great many colourful tattoos and ear piercings in triplicate. She wears a lot of blacks and has big red lace-up boots. She asked me to teach her to knit and to sew, so in exchange for some help at the allotment, I agreed to do so.

She makes commemorative items for and about her son. He died when he was two. It left a hole in her heart. I think she is trying to sew it up so it doesn't feel so much pain. She is obsessed about embroidery and although her attire is starkly coloured, she loves every colour of the rainbow in thread. She is not very talkative. Sewing is how she expresses herself. When she is absorbed in her work, I see in her a deep concentration. Where nothing at school could keep her attention, this old-fashioned and feminine art captivates her mind.

I told Alice about the fox, one day on the allotment when she was digging a bed for me to plant some sweet potatoes. She looked up and almost smiled. She does that a lot. I guess it's hard for her to smile fully after what happened to her son. Bottled up sadness has a way of doing that. I had a lot of that after gran passed away, especially after I found the love letters in her attic from a man who wasn't my grandfather.

We all have secrets, I reasoned, but it wasn't any good. The sadness felt like a lake of tears inside that needed to be shed but was frozen instead and wouldn't emerge. Perhaps this is similar to how Alice feels, betrayed by her son leaving her, who should have grown up healthy and strong like herself. It's a mysterious thing, loss, and how it affects us all differently.

Alice wanted to see the fox, so one afternoon, we brought a flask of tea and some biscuits and sat in the deckchairs at the back of the allotment and waited, but no fox appeared. Instead, a ginger cat arrived who wove around Alice's legs as if he knew her. Rubbing his chin against her boots and yawning on his back at her feet. I looked at the pendant on his collar, inscribed with the name Billy, the same name as her son. This cat only visited when Alice was there and never at any other time. He followed her around and grew strong on the fishy treats she brought for him.

Around about November, he stopped visiting. We were preparing the allotment for the winter and putting down the groundsheets to prevent weeds from taking over. Alice had some news for me. She was pregnant. I made the point of hugging her and she smiled.

She suggested I teach her how to make some baby clothes. I had a few patterns but I wasn't sure she could manage them on her own. She asked if there was a pattern for a christening gown. I said I would look. She told me she would like me to be the baby's godparent. I must say I was very touched. No student of mine had ever thought that highly of me before. She said that when it was older, I could teach the child everything I knew about knitting and embroidery, even if it was born a boy.

Alice wintered alone. It was too cold for any of us to go out. And in the spring the baby was born: a boy. She called me up soon after the birth and said that I could come over and see her and the infant. I took her one of my experimental cakes and plenty of yarn that I had squirrelled away in the attic for a rainy day. It was pure linen, the finest quality.

Billy the cat never showed up at the allotment again. Perhaps he had found a more fruitful stomping ground. One fine June day, the fox returned, with two almost grown pups in tow. They stayed awhile at my feet, playing. It was as if the fox wanted me to see her handiwork, her beautiful offspring. Then they left, never to be seen again, not by me at least.

The sweet potatoes came up year after year, even though I had never planted any more after the first harvest. It was a mystery how it happened, that the soil was so fertile despite the fact I refused to use any kind of fertilizer on the ground. I never had a failed crop. And although Alice visited less and less, because she was busy bringing up her son, I felt I had renewed strength to work the ground myself.

I grew foods for brain health and longevity, like purple potatoes and red cabbage. Soon my allotment became a medicinal garden full of herbs and exotic fruit and vegetables. The plum and hazelnut trees always produced a bumper harvest. And as for the apple tree that I planted from a pip, there were never any worms in the apples ever again. Even the bitter radishes and sour rhubarb tasted sweet and made their way into my cakes and savouries. 'Savouries' is a good word, as it comprises the word 'savour'. And that is what I learned to do, with every moment left for me to enjoy.

Short Stories – Chapter 2 – Alice with Golden Thread

I am taking him some pumpkin pie today, from a pumpkin that I have grown at my friend Eloise's allotment. It has to go through a metal detector before the prisoner is allowed to receive my parcel. The prisoner is called Rick.

I started visiting the prison as a volunteer when my second son, Ryan, started nursery. I needed something to do with my days and as I was embroidering so many things anyway, and had learned so much from Eloise, I was encouraged to pass on my skills to others. At first, I was very nervous about how violent the inmates were and what they would make of me. But apart from the odd fight that erupted between themselves, they were pretty tame, all things considered. I wasn't exactly sure how many of the prisoners were there for violent offences. We volunteers were told the bare minimum of their crimes, in order that we treat them as naturally and as normally as we could.

I have a problem with some words. Take the word 'normal' for instance. One person's normal is another person's 'way-out'. In the case of getting tattoos, my conservative parents thought it was a bit too way out of their comfort zone. But one person's comfort zone is another person's prison.

The purpose of teaching the prisoners embroidery was to help them plan something and see it through to the end. And the embroidery needles in question might have been a welcome relief from heroin needles, that in some cases would have been the only kind of needles they'd have known before.

The prisoner allocated to me, Rick, was in for drug offences. He got 18 months and still had another 8 to serve. If he had good behaviour counted in his favour, the prison authorities might shave 2-3 months off his sentence duration. He was keen to behave well, in the prison wardens' eyes at any rate. He's had enough of being confined.

You could tell Rick hadn't had much of an education. He wasn't confident with words. He mumbled with a bowed head and called me Miss. I insisted he tried to remember to call me Alice. I told him that he and I were really no different, that we wanted to make good with our lives and stay out of trouble. He smiled a smile that seemed to have some kind of a grudge behind it, curling his lip up to reveal a gap where an incisor should have been. Next to this gap was a gold tooth that glinted like pirate treasure.

When he saw that I had noticed it he said defensively, "I paid for this tooth, legit, like." I nodded and pointed back to his embroidery to encourage him not to become distracted and lose concentration and to continue with embroidering the important things from his life that he was sewing onto a piece of linen. Then one day, he came out with it, the joke that made me smile. Not a sad, corner of the mouth smile, but a big smile that was threatening to turn into a downright chuckle.

"Embroidery really suits my life," Rick said one day. I was glad that he wasn't mumbling so much anymore.

"Oh yes, how so?" I enquired, pleased that he felt these lessons had some meaning for him.

"Cause I embroidered the truth in the law court before they sentenced me. I'm only here because of embroidery."

I fought with my smile not to turn into a chuckle because when I do laugh, I tend to sound like a gruff old man who's smoked one too many cigars.

"Well," I said, "I think that's a different type of embroidery you hopefully won't be using again." I tried winking at him in a friendly manner but he asked if I had something in my eye. He could remove it if I liked, he said. I quickly changed the subject. Prisoners and volunteers were not allowed to touch.

The first thing Rick embroidered was his mother on her deathbed, and him aged three at her bedside crying a big tear in blue thread.

"Young Rick looks awfully sad," I said. "I know what sadness looks like," I added in a whisper.

"I wish I'd had something nice to give her, in the hospital, but I was empty-handed." Rick sniffed and wiped his nose on the back of his sleeve, leaving a silvery trail like slug slime along the fabric. We have more than enough slugs to know what to do with down at the allotment but I didn't want to be thinking about them right now.

"I have a cold," said Rick, by way of explanation.

"Why not embroider some flowers in your hand that you are giving to your mum, and turn her mouth up into a smile."

"I like the way you're thinking," he said and did just as I had told him.

The next time we met, I'm sure I could detect that he was lighter and less heavy of mind. Someone had brought him some fresh flowers that were in a plastic container on the table. They were the same colours as the ones he had embroidered the week before. His gold tooth glinted quite a few times that day until we got onto another episode in his life. It was when he was beaten up in the school playground. He drew a big fist and a black eye crying red tears, and the word 'CRUNCH' in red thread.

"Peace is better than fighting," I said.

"Yes, Miss, I wish I'd had him in pieces," he replied sadly.

"Not that kind of peace," I said, shaking my head. "The kind of peace that makes your heart glad."

"You mean the kind of peace I'll feel when I'm a dad?"

"I'm not sure having kids is going to be very peaceful, but um, maybe the peace you'll feel just after the baby is born."

"I'm gonna pay for him to learn Kung Fu, to keep him out of trouble. No one would mess with him and if they do, he'd chop them into a pulp." Rick said.

"The best defence when threatened is always running away," I said.

So he embroidered his future son as a great runner with lots of medals and a dove of peace above his head, protecting him.

The next visit was cancelled – Rick had been punched in the stomach by a fellow inmate and was resting a bruised rib. Luckily, he later told me, in an animated description of events, the gloopy prison food in his stomach had cushioned the blow. I was proud of him that he'd not retaliated. The attacker got another two months inside. Rick's peaceful reaction was duly noted and commended by the prison staff.

"I'd have run away if I could've," he said on my next visit. "But there's nowhere to run to in here except back to the cell." He embroidered his prison cell but turned it into a cave with a roasted pig on a spit. The analogy wasn't lost on me. The police hadn't been his greatest allies in life, being from the wrong side of the tracks, as he was.

"Perhaps you have to think about leaving your cave one day," I said. "Why don't you embroider what you want your future to look like?" The tooth glinted gold as he told me in great detail his dreams and ambitions. He embroidered the family recipe pizza from the pizzeria he was going to run, the small terraced house he would buy in a quiet street away from the drug dealers. Then he embroidered himself with a black cape and mortarboard hat after he got his degree through night school. The family he would have, and his proud father. Finally, he wanted to embroider an image of me, giving him the homemade pumpkin pie that would feature among the recipes of his restaurant of homespun cooking. Among the embroidery materials was a small piece of gold-coloured thread. He embroidered a halo above my head. It made me chuckle, a real old-man-who-smoked-too-many-cigars kind of chuckle.

"Miss, you never told me you had such a dirty laugh," he said. "I might have to replace this halo of yours with two horns." But he was only joking, thankfully.

Eloise and I celebrated the day Rick was released from prison. Several years later he arrived at my front door on a bicycle with three large pizzas I had ordered for a party. He looked like a man who wasn't embroidering the truth any more to try and get out of trouble. It looked as if he'd left trouble way behind and it was never going to catch him up again. I don't think he recognised me because of my silly party wig and fancy dress, but when he saw the embroidery on the wall in the hall as I opened the door, recognition shot through his eyes with the warmth of a thousand fireflies over a moonlit lake. There was a glint of gold and he was gone. As he cycled up the street he stopped and turned and shouted back: "Miss Alice, I love your Cruella de Ville outfit! It really suits you!"

"Thanks a lot!" I shouted back. "I'm dressed as Crystal from Dynasty."

"I knew that. I really did, "he called back with an embarrassed grin. "It's the tattoos, they made you look a bit severe."

"You can talk, with that gold tooth," I said.

"Don't let everyone know, or they'll all want one," he replied. "Hey," I called out. "Good luck with everything, mate."

"You too, sweet lady," he said before cycling off into the distance.

The pizza tasted great. I encouraged everyone at the party to write some good reviews for his website. I saw Rick from time to time, clearing tables and scrubbing floors at his pizza place. It looked a bit run-down and in need of a modern refit. He was thinner than before. It really seemed like he couldn't even afford to eat his own pizzas. He must have got a bank loan because one day I saw he had an advert running in the local cinema before the movie began. The advert jingle ran: "Rick's pizza: the best pizza on earth. Well, probably." I was glad to see he was sticking to the truth without too much embroidery on top of it. His pizzas really were the best pizzas on earth, though. I could vouch for that.

When my cousin left school, he got a summer job at Rick's pizza place. He used his bicycle to ferry around the pizzas and advertising leaflets. Then a famous soap star was pictured at the pizzeria enjoying a lavish meal with his wife and three kids. That image was splashed across the tabloids. It made Rick's place very popular for a while, especially among the school kids who watched the show, but then the interest died down. As with many teenage interests, it was only a fad. But it was when Rick's aunt was visiting from abroad that things really turned around for the better. She brought along her own recipes for pasta and pesto sauce. She never revealed the secret ingredients but the taste was addictive and sales shot through the roof.

A supermarket took an interest and decided to manufacture the sauces on a grand scale. Soon Rick's aunt had enough money to become a partner in the restaurant and pay for some proper classy advertising in the paper. The single establishment in time then became a small chain with updated decor that made for a great atmosphere. I was really proud of how far Rick had come and how hard he'd worked. Things couldn't have been easy.

He invited me to his wedding and I shed a tear when the vows were exchanged. As a present, I'd made the happy couple some embroidery, with embellishments, framed in a gold-coloured frame, the same shade as Rick's tooth. He told me they'd put it in the nursery when the twins arrived. I bet Rick's kids will have his father's gutsy determination. Perhaps when they're older, Rick can teach them some embroidery, the kind that won't get them into any trouble.

Chapter 3 – The Music Box

Every Saturday I work in the antiques shop up the High Road. It's opposite Rick's Pizza Place and squeezed between the 24-hour supermarket on the left and the chemist on the right. I say 'squeezed' for a reason. This is an old Elizabethan shop, with a droopy roof, small doors, and bay windows. It's a listed building but that means that it's historically interesting but not very practical by today's standards. The three steps into the main entrance frustrate many a person with pram or trolley, and it's totally inaccessible to wheelchair-users.

This bothers me quite a bit, how history is put before functionality. Even the stairs that twist up to the first and second floors are exceptionally narrow, making people of a certain girth unable to navigate this building. Sometimes, American or Japanese tourists will pop into the shop to have a look at the beams across the ceiling. They might leave with a small souvenir of their visit: a Victorian tile, or precious stone, or enamelled brooch. Something they can easily pack inside a suitcase without much bother.

This week I sold a Georgian commode. You'd be surprised at what people buy. It was very ornate, I must admit, with inlaid wood and a secret compartment for God knows what. Perhaps the whole thing was just a fancy safe in disguise. I like to imagine what the minds were like of the people who previously owned the objects in this shop. I bet each item has a story to tell if only it could speak, but sadly these stories were lost to time and place many moons ago.

I've lived in this area for decades and I've seen people and shops come and go. But this one's been here as long as I can remember. My mother Betty used to pick me up so I could look into the window in awe at the trinkets inside. She told me that the objects in the shop were once owned by wealthy folks who lived a long time ago and who are now long dead, and that these objects are bought today by even richer living folks wanting something special to leave their children after they die. I asked mum if she would leave me something after she died. She asked me if I knew what the word 'die' meant. I said I could die for an ice-cream right now. Then you shall have one, me little angel, she said, pinching my cheek and leading me by the hand to the ice-cream parlour around the corner. It had 101 flavours but I only ever chose the one: mango and lime.

Mum used to sing to me in her kimono-style dressing gown that had a design of pink blossom on it. She called me her little cherry pie. When she was out, I would put on her high heels and dressing gown and swish it about the floor, trying to look attractive, as attractive as any 4-year-old boy could look with lipstick on his face in all the wrong places.

My dad, Henry, was a gambler but at least he didn't drink. He liked to keep a clean and sober head for when he played poker. He won quite a bit of dosh, but then blew it all on the races, going on some silly hunch he had that he felt compelled to follow. When his gambling days were done, thanks to some hypnotherapy his brother fixed up for him, he opened a grocer's shop where Rick's Pizza Place now stands. Every Wednesday on my way back from school dad would give me some cabbage leaves to feed the ducks at the local park. I wouldn't have thought it was that good for them, but that was dad all over, always wanting to help out in any way he could, without really thinking things through for the best.

At the back of the antiques shop are all the finest things. The items too pricey or delicate to be out front for customers to see. These go to auction every month with bidders from around the world. I have to be very careful when visiting the loo, not to bump into any of these priceless items. Saturdays are the busiest time of the week. That's why I prefer to work on this day. The shop's owners, Doris and Pat, like me out front where the customers can interact with me. They say my calm and friendly disposition helps draw them in to spend a lot more dosh than they otherwise would do. It's kind of Doris to pay me on commission. On some Saturdays, I can earn as much as £200.

It's only Betty and me at home now, and most days she has trouble getting out of her chair, which she'll she'll hardly attempt anyway except to switch the radio on or visit the lav. I'm her main carer, though we have someone to visit while I'm at work to cook her a meal and bath her. She, Betty, that is, and I like to sing in the evenings, she with her glass of sherry to open up her appetite, and me with my honey and lemon tea that soothes my vocal cords.

Mum has played opera to me ever since I was a child. She says I'm a great singer, that I have a natural gift. She'd love for me to sing in public but I'm too shy. I only feel comfortable singing in front of mum. She's very patient with me. Even if she's having a bad day and is in lots of pain, she never grumbles. I might see a wince or two as she slowly moves about the house, but that's all. But I know how tired she is. I can see her eyes are in some distant place, unable to tune into me when I'm there. But she still loves to hear me sing.

Last year she was diagnosed with cancer that was at quite a late stage. It was devastating for us both. The doctors tried chemo on her and it looked promising at first but the cancer was aggressive and had already spread to a few other parts of her body. I know it's only a matter of months that we'll be together so I try to spend as much time with her as possible but she insisted I keep my Saturday job and shouldn't be worrying about her so much. Even if I go out for some groceries, which doesn't take long, I fear she will have passed away while I am gone. I want to be there when it happens. I don't want her to die alone.

In her more lucid moments, Betty tells me I could have been a great opera singer, and still can if I put my mind to it. I'm okay with one or two people in the shop, but the thought of a whole audience in front of me gives me the wobbles. Shaky knees are my problem. Sometimes when I'm alone in the shop and there is a temporary lull in the customers, I break into song. The place has great acoustics, with a resonant echo, especially in the back of the shop. It was there that I shattered a very expensive piece of Edwardian glassware, one day a few weeks ago as I was getting my coat on and about to lock up.

I had no idea I could hit such a perfect high note. I'm lucky the windows didn't break. When I told Doris, she laughed and said the insurance would cover the cost of the glass, but that I wasn't to sing anymore. I was glad she took it so well. I could easily have lost my job.

A few days later, a young man came into the shop looking for an engagement present for his partner. After chatting for a while, I recommended to him a beautiful music box inlaid with mother of pearl. I didn't even need to play it for him – he took my word for it that it was a very beautiful and romantic tune. On the look of the thing alone, he bought it for £400. Several weeks later he returned to the shop, with the item wrapped up in a scarf. He looked beaten down somehow.

He asked for his money back and when I asked why, he said that at their lavish engagement party, his fiancée had opened the music box and instead of a beautiful tune, a loud high-pitched note had rung out, shattering all the glasses and the chandelier. There was red wine and shards of glass everywhere. People screamed. One person fainted. Unfortunately, that person had been his future mother-in-law, and the engagement was called off. His fiancée had seen it all as a bad omen and refused to marry him.

I think you're better off without her, I said. He gave me a weak smile and said he'd given up on women for the time being. He was focusing on his golf swing instead. I took the music box and wound the key. I tentatively opened it but all that issued was the beautiful melody I had been familiar with before. The gentleman looked puzzled. I said I was terribly sorry I couldn't give him a refund but that as a goodwill gesture I could give him £50 to spend in the shop another time. He took the voucher thankfully and wrapped the music box in the scarf and left.

The following week, the gentleman came back, he said his name was Christopher, and would I care to join him for a dinner at Rick's Pizza Place after work. I said, well, yes, that would be nice and that I shut up the shop at 6.30 pm. I called Betty's carer to ask if she could stay a few more hours and it was all settled. Mum had shown signs of some improvement and she insisted I go on this date with my young man, as she put it. Christopher was there on the dot. Not many people were at Rick's pizzeria that evening. We practically had it all to ourselves. We sat in one of the romantic booths for courting couples and we shared a large pizza. Strangely our favourite toppings were all the same: chicken, pineapple, mushrooms, and spinach.

He said he owned a racehorse called Lone Ranger. I couldn't believe I was mixing with what my mother would call a posh person in spiffy garb who was flash with his cash. To Betty, I must seem like the complete opposite by comparison – one of the common people. But she always told me that was nothing to be ashamed of. By an accident of birth, some have more than others. Mum wanted me to close that gap by becoming a famous singer. But there were things Betty didn't know about me. My real dream was to buy a camper van and travel around the world.

But now, instead, in this candle-lit restaurant, I saw myself on a motorbike, with Christopher in the sidecar, travelling through country lanes. Going to the races every Saturday, and buying some of the antiques from the shop I'd worked in for twelve years without a day off sick. But was that the life I actually wanted? It was a pleasant dream for a few seconds, but mum needed me now and I still needed her. To be with Christopher in any long-term meaningful way was unfeasible, an unbelievable prospect. I made my excuses and left. Politely, mind, for it's never good to be rude if one can help it, as mum always taught me.

Two months later mum died. She had been very weak and I was beside her at the time. Opera was playing softly on the radio. Her last words to me were, 'Sing for the people, my darling boy'. I was in a state of grief for many weeks, just numb. Then it began to properly sink in and her dying wish came back to my mind over and over like a refrain. The house was up for sale quite soon after she passed. I just wanted to get away from all the painful memories of her sickness and not be reminded of her so much. I wanted, however difficult it would be, to move on.

I had to reduce the price of the house twice before anyone bought it. They were a young couple with a baby on the way looking for their first-time home. Before I finally moved out into the second-hand camper van parked outside that I'd bought with the little money mum had left me from years of saving and being frugal while dad was still alive, I received a parcel in the post. It was from Christopher. He'd got my address from Doris in the shop. He'd sent me the antique music box and a note saying: "In memory of the lovely evening I spent with you. I've been tinkering with the mechanics of it with you in mind. It works differently now, I think you'll approve." There was also an invitation to his wedding – a wedding with two grooms and no bride. I was happy for him. He asked if I would sing at the reception as I had told him of my ability with music. I wrote a postcard back, saying I was flattered but that I'd be halfway across Europe by then. I wished him luck.

He rang and left a message on my answerphone a few days later. Take a chance on the Lone Ranger, Saturday, Grand National. I put £100 on it and with its odds, if I'd won, I would've had enough petrol money for the whole year. However, it came in last. Something in the crowd had spooked it and it had bolted like a wild stallion. It was probably for the best. I had my dad's gift for picking the wrong horse. I saw it as a warning not to gamble again. Although trekking around Europe in a camper van was a gamble of sorts. One that I desperately wanted to pay off if my plan worked.

It was hard to say goodbye to Doris and Pat, but they'd already found a bubbly and attractive young girl to replace me on the Saturday shift. I just hope she doesn't sing opera, I said. Pat smiled and said she didn't think that was likely.

I decided I had to honour my mum's dying wish as a way to remember the good times together and keep them alive. So I turned my camper van into a travelling opera stage. I even attached some red velvet curtains for a suitable theatrical effect. Up and down the country in every coastal town, I gave performances. But kids on the beach weren't interested in Opera. They preferred the funfair and the sideshows. Punch and Judy on the beach was their preference. It was hard to interest the crowd when I had no backing music and I was still feeling the nerves.

I took the music box with me wherever I went, but I never played it in case it would backfire and send out that piercingly shrill note that might shatter the windows on my van. I've no idea where that music box came from originally, but one evening when I was cleaning the base, I rubbed away some black polish to reveal the words, *To my darling Betty, from Henry, may the music always be with you and our beautiful son. May 12th, 1836.* Chills ran up and down my spine. Henry and Betty had been my parents' names, but they of course had not been born until much later. And May 12th was my birthday. The universe works in mysterious ways, my mother always said. I looked up at the stars where I was sure she was looking down on me. It surely does, I thought and let the words be carried out of my mind and away on the breeze to some other time and place that connected her to me.

Something like a soft voice whispering in my head told me to go into the forest with the music box and play it. So that is what I did. What emerged was the tune of my favourite opera, but each time I wound up the box and opened it another opera would play, absent of the lead singer's voice. It was a remarkable thing. Christopher must have some special abilities beyond my knowledge. Whatever he had done to the music box had rendered it almost magical. I saw it as I sign I must go to the place of the heart of opera: Italy. I would start my journey in the morning. The world, that is, my world, felt as if it was glowing with a thousand different possibilities. Maybe Italy would have the answers I sought and provide the life I wanted. Only time would tell. I used to think that any kind of a different life from what I had would be impossible to achieve. But today I remembered the quote from Audrey Hepburn that the word 'Impossible' is just the words 'I'm possible' if looked at another way. Mum would've liked that. She was always telling me to trust myself more. She said I had good instincts. Just maybe not at the races. I had to start somewhere. Amalfi seemed as good a place as any.

Chapter 4 – Amalfi On My Mind

I arrive at the beach as the dawn light settles over the town. The buildings that go up a steep incline cut into the rock of a small hill overlooking the sea, have their plasterwork tinted pink by the sun. The air is cool now but it'll soon be hot enough for me to take off my tweed waistcoat, the one thing I brought with me that belonged to dad. Betty kept it all these years. It's such a good bit of cloth with an excellent weave, she told me after he died. She liked to take it out now and then and look at it and feel the soft wool under her fingers and get lost in memories of him.

I thought it might bring me a bit of luck, taking it with me; maybe not on the races, but there were other kinds of good fortune to be had. I wish I believed in something more reliable than good old-fashioned luck, but mum and dad had never been ones for organised religion. When mum died, I did pray for her. I walked into a church, sat down in a pew, and prayed. It can't do any harm, I'd thought. It did make me feel better, but only for as long as I was there. When I left, the gloomy thoughts returned.

But if it hadn't been for the sorrow, I wouldn't have propelled myself out of our small town with my camper van and into the great unknown. Gradually my comfort zone expanded, and what was scary at first became more ordinary. The British coast wasn't much of a success for me regarding the singing, but here I am in Amalfi with its small, bright, hopeful buildings woven into the hillside near the beach. Things are looking up. And I'm a lot more relaxed.

It's a popular tourist destination. The town square with a decorative fountain, the small shops and cafes, and the grand hotels resemble those of many other coastal towns. Yet, something about Amalfi makes me feel very much at home. Perhaps in another time and place, my soul had been born an Italian and lived in this very place. It all seems strangely familiar, like a feeling of having been here before. On several occasions, I knew what was going to be around a particular street corner. Perhaps these were memories from some bygone era resurfacing.

Betty wouldn't have been surprised. She believed in reincarnation. She said she and Henry had also been married in a past life. It'd been their destiny to meet in this one. And I hope it's part of my destiny to be here now. I sit on a bench with my cheese sandwich and thermos, looking out to sea. It's a calm day, the waves are gentle, and the breeze is light. A few people are walking along the jetty: a girl with a massive backpack who can't be more than about 15; an elderly couple that walk slowly and stooped as if every joint in their fragile old frames causes them pain. But at least they have the view. They still have that, and each other too. That's something.

Today I'll be singing in a hotel foyer as the guests assemble for lunch. It's quite a grand hotel on the seafront with freshly painted white shutters on every large window. Flavio, the hotel manager, heard me singing in the town square and must have taken pity on me. I'm glad he did. Any opportunity to sing for an audience is better than none.

The young girl with the backpack is looking at me intently and I find her gaze uncomfortable. It's like she's trying to search my mind for something she's lost. I hope she's not in any trouble. I can't afford to get tangled up in someone else's problems right now, which sounds selfish of me, I know, but hey, I'm here for other reasons than to be someone's shoulder to cry on. I'm here for me and Betty and Henry and Christopher and Doris and Pat and even for Rick of the pizza place fame. I'm here to put our little town on the map if I can.

I throw the sandwich wrapper in the bin, walk to the central fountain and refill my thermos. A couple of children are having a water pistol fight and I get caught in the crossfire. My shirt is soaked. I frown and waggle my finger at them comically. They laugh and run off towards the beach, awkward with their flip-flops and ungainly long limbs.

The sky is an intense blue with motionless clouds suspended in it. I look for some meaning or symbols in the shapes but find none except something resembling a small boat with a sail. Mum used to be able to see all kinds of things in the clouds. For her, it was like reading tealeaves. She could weave whole stories from what she saw there. But my mind was always elsewhere and only half-listening. Looking at the insects in the grass going about their business, oblivious to all of us. Ladybirds were my favourite. The pepper-red wings and black spots were beautiful to me.

A large beetle lands on my white shirt. It has luminous green iridescent wings. It craws along, perhaps attracted by the water stain. I let it rest and take a drink before it flies off again and continues its search. The clouds catch my eye again. According to Henry, this was where the angels lived. I can't see any right now so perhaps they're invisible but I still get the sense of a benevolent presence watching over me.

I'm back on the beachfront now. The elderly couple have gone but the backpacker girl is fishing out something from her rucksack, an apple, I think. She has cropped blond hair and looks very boyish in her dark blue T-shirt and brown shorts. I wonder what brought her to Amalfi. Does she have dreams to fulfil just like I do? Or could she be a teenage runaway? She must sense my eyes on her because she looks up suddenly and waves. I give her a thumbs-up. I have an urge to start singing to her but think better of it. There's a time and a place for everything and now isn't the time or the place to break into song, I tell myself.

The heat is rising. Gulls swoop low and cry out. They sound fierce, demanding, on edge. Or maybe it's me that's on edge, knowing I really have to make a go of this or it'll be back to London for me and to full-time work, maybe in the antiques shop, maybe at Rick's pizzeria. I can't do much else but sing. I rest on the sand, going through my performance in my head, and go back to my campervan and do a rehearsal. Then it's nearly lunchtime.

I put on some clean clothes and a bow tie, red velvet, a gift from my dad for my 21st birthday. It gives me a confidence boost. I feel as if he and Betty are here in some way, rooting for me. My silver cufflinks were a parting gift from Doris and Pat. They're Edwardian antique, each inlaid with a square of mother-of-pearl that glints when they catch the light. I give my smart shoes a final polish with a hanky and I'm ready. I gently pick up my music box, wind it up and knock on it three times for good luck. Three is the magic number, Betty used to say. I feel something tingling in my throat.

I hope it's not a cold coming on. I swallow a spoonful of honey and then set off for The Hotel Resplendent.

The foyer is plush: red carpets with a gold fleur-de-lis pattern, candelabras fixed to the walls, and large mirrors with ornate gold frames. Up above, dangling elegantly from the high ceiling, hangs a chandelier that catches the light and sparkles like a cloud full of diamonds. Maybe that's the kind of cloud the angels make their home in. There's a bench beside a mirror that's in a mock renaissance style. I take a seat with my music box beside me and wait for Flavio to arrive.

"Welcome, welcome," he says, as if he's doubly happy to see me.

"I'm a little nervous," I say.

"Just sing like you sang in the square by the fountain. Forget the audience. Think only of the song." Flavio is right, I need to focus on the words alone. I feel reassured and the tremble in my knees lessens.

He ushers me to a spot in front of the largest floor-to-ceiling mirror and gently commands me to begin. I open the music box and the music from Puccini's Turandot emanates. It's as if the whole orchestra is present. I begin to sing 'Nessun Dorma', the notes coming out pure and true, my throat vibrating and my chest filled with energy. Guests arrive and linger to hear me. Soon there are so many that Flavio has to encourage some to take a seat at lunch in the restaurant beyond the foyer. They are reluctant to leave, however.

Next, I sing from Verdi's Rigoletto 'La Donne e Mobile.' More people gather in the foyer, whispering excitedly to each other, craning for a view. But I'm barely aware of the crowd. I'm lost in my own world, carried along by the flow of the music issuing from my music box. When the recital is over, there's a round of applause. They want an encore so I sing 'Che gelida manina' from La Boheme. I sing with such tender emotion even I didn't know I was capable of, that a lady in the audience wipes away a tear. I feel privileged to have moved someone so much with my singing. Betty would've been proud.

Finally, it's over and I'm transported back to this foyer in Amalfi. Flavio pats me on the back and hands me the liras he promised me.

"I'll call you if I require a singer again," he says. "This is a rare occurrence at our Hotel. Entertainments don't come cheap. The place needs repairs. I'll have to consider it carefully."

There are no fanfares, no definite offers of more work. It is just a straightforward business transaction. And now it's over, with this polite brush-off. I try to keep my disappointment from showing. If there'll be no regular work here, I'll have to think of something else. Outside, I rest my music box on a wall as I tie my shoelace that's come undone. Someone brushes past me. I look up. The music box is gone. The street is crowded with people milling about in every direction. I don't know who to follow or where to turn. I'm nothing without that music box.

Then I see her in the distance, running. It's the backpack girl only this time her backpack is gone. There's nothing for it, I have to chase after her. It's the only lead I have and I must follow. I set off, building my pace as I get going, but she outruns me. She turns corners and dodges people swiftly, as if she's done this countless times before. She's nothing but a common thief!

I'm getting out of breath. All that singing was strenuous enough and now this running is taking more of a toll. I really should cut down on those cheese sandwiches. And I shouldn't have done that encore. Expressing so much emotion is tiring. I stop and lean against a wall to get my breath back. My heart is pounding. I see the girl dart into an alley and she's gone. I've lost her now. And I've lost my precious music box too. Damn! I've got no puff left in me so I stroll miserably back to the beach near where my campervan is parked. I try and get a grip on my racing thoughts and my anger. That girl was only interested in what she could steal from me. No wonder she was so friendly, so that I would let my guard down.

What'll I do without my precious box of a thousand tunes? It's not like any other object I know. A whole orchestra encapsulated within the magical wood. It might as well have been made of gold and diamonds, for all it meant to me. That scruffy girl – that greedy good-for-nothing stray! I feel the anger rising to my flushed, hot cheeks. If I could get my hands on her, I'd spit in her eye. I'm shaking now. My dreams are shattered into a million pieces.

Or maybe something else is going on here. I'm sure the girl wouldn't have done this out of spite. She must've needed the money she was hoping to get for the box. She probably doesn't even have any idea how much it means to me, how my livelihood depends on it. I would've just given her some money if she'd asked. She must be in a lot of trouble to do this.

Then I feel a tap on my shoulder and I turn. It's her, standing there, not at all out of breath from running like the wind, and with the music box in her hands.

"I saw the thief dash off with your wooden box," she says. "I wasn't going to let him get away with that, was I?"

"What? You rescued my music box?"

"Yeah."

"Thank you so much, from the bottom of my heart. You don't know how much this box means to me," I say, still breathless. I am so relieved. The anger and tension I've been feeling evaporate like steam. I examine the box. It isn't even scuffed. She's beaming from ear to ear to have rescued it for me.

"Don't go losing that thing again, will you? I won't be around to rescue it next time," she grins. "I've got to get my things and be off. Well, nice knowing you." She doffs an imaginary hat and heads off to fetch her backpack that's still on a nearby bench where she'd left it. Not only was she not a thief at all but a brave girl, and a selfless one too. She risked all of her belongings being stolen for the sake of recapturing my music box.

I must've been so focused on her that I failed to see the person she'd been running after.

I tell her: "Thank you so much for your help. Can I buy you lunch?" But she declines.

"I have to be on my way, I have a boat to catch," she tells me.

I offer her some liras as a reward for her valiant effort and she takes them gratefully.

"What's your name?" I ask.

"Devon," she says.

"Good luck on your travels," I say.

"And you on yours too, " she replies, and gives me the thumbs-up sign and I return it. She heads off into the crowd, just another one of the milling throng, but one I'll never forget.

I feel a little ashamed I mistook her for a thief. That'll teach me to try and see the bigger picture instead of being intensely focused only on one small detail. My hot temper can get the better of me if I'm not careful. Too much fire in the blood, mum used to say. But then that very thing is what I bring to the singing. The fire of emotion but tamed and channelled for the good.

Then I realise I've lost one of my cufflinks so I retrace my steps to The Hotel Resplendent. The foyer is empty except for a lone gentleman at reception who is settling his bill. He is well dressed and a little old-fashioned looking. He wears a waistcoat and smart, pressed trousers and sports an elegant cane to lean on. It makes him look extremely dapper and a little out of place at this seaside resort. His moustache is a thing of wonder and if he had a top hat he'd look Edwardian. But I mustn't get too distracted. I resume my search for the missing cufflink, but it's gone, nowhere to be found. So I did lose something today after all.

However, the man approaches me and offers me his card.

"I own a fleet of cruise ships that leave from Salerno port and sail around Italy," he says. I'm wondering where this conversation is headed.

Perhaps he is looking for customers. But then he asks: "Would you be interested to sing on board for the passengers as part of their entertainment package? A six-month contract to begin with and more bookings if it goes well." I'm stunned.

"What, you want me to sing on your ship?" I ask, incredulously.

'Yes, if you have no prior engagements."

"Thank you, sir, so very much, thank you, thank you," I gush.

"It's you I must thank for your magnificent singing. When my wife was moved to tears earlier I knew I had to book you on one of my ships. The next one leaves in seven days and you must be ready by then."

"Of course," I say. "Sir, you can count on me."

Before I leave he says: "By any chance are you looking for this?" He hands me the missing cufflink, fished out of his pocket. I take it gratefully.

My cufflinks and I and my music box are back together and we're heading out on a real adventure into the unknown. I'd better get my sea legs ready and refuel my transportation. No more cheese sandwiches. The first class owner of the ship has told me I'll be entitled to third-class accommodation and food aboard The Valiant Prince, the cruise liner I'm to be working in. I sit down in the campervan, clasp my hands together, and pray. This time it's a prayer of thanks. I thank providence and the girl with the legs that can run like the wind. I thank Henry and Betty; and Doris and Pat for giving me the cufflinks with the loose fitting. If I hadn't have lost one, I'd never have gone back to the hotel and met the gentlemanly owner of ships. Now I know what the symbol of the boat was that I saw earlier in the clouds: a premonition of my future.

Before I leave Amalfi, I make one last trip. I visit the fountain in the town square and throw a few lira into the water. I make a wish because now I believe that wishes can come true. I buy some food for the journey; some nuts and olives, and bread. I've come a long way to be here and my story has barely even begun. I feel sad to be leaving the place and I vow to return one day, after I have sailed the world and sung my heart out. For this is where I would like to settle and make roots.

Chapter 5 _ The Chandelier of Stars

I've worked at The Hotel Resplendent for 14 years now, since 1894, and I'm the sort of person that just blends into the background. That's how I know I'm doing my job well. The receptionist isn't meant to draw too much attention to themselves. Even my uniform has been chosen so that I blend into the surroundings. The burgundy fabric with gold braids around the cuffs and lapels, and gold buttons down the front and on the pockets, just like the buttons on the elevator and the burgundy flock wallpaper in the foyer. At all times I have the appearance of being cool, calm and collected, but it's only on the surface. Underneath the exterior, like a duck, I'm furiously paddling to stay afloat.

Nobody would know it to look at me, that I'm actually a very nervous person who finds talking to strangers extremely challenging. I trained for a couple of years in the theatre but my career as an actress led nowhere. There just weren't the parts for people who looked like me. This olive complexion of a gypsy, my frame, short and stooped, with big eyes and infernally bushy eyebrows. I could play a pantomime villain in England, but in Italy? They prefer the beauties here.

However, my acting skills were first rate. And I still use them today. What I really think and believe must remain hidden under the surface or I would lose my job. I have to be the epitome of consideration and respect because that is how this hotel would like to appear according to its owner, Flavio, who is my boss.

I get to know the visitors a little. They often confide in me certain of their likes and dislikes. Something they want brought their room, or something they want removed from it because it bothers them. The wrong kind of soap with a fragrance they find distasteful, or a drinks cabinet with an annoyingly creaky hinge, all have to be replaced or attended to. The wife of one visiting dignitary insisted that I find her a pair of slippers made of mink. With my connections it is possible for me to find almost anything that the visitors request. But even for me, mink slippers were a little beyond my capabilities.

I like to be of service to the clientele in any way that I can, be it providing hazelnut gelato in the early hours just beyond midnight, or a goldfish in a bowl to someone who finds it relaxing to watch it swim about as they drop off to sleep. I understand that these people are far from home and anything that makes them feel more comfortable and value their stay here is what I am here to provide.

But of all the things about them, it is the clients' jewellery that I take the most interest in. There are pearls, diamonds, rubies and sapphires, in every intricate design that you could possibly imagine. I have the job of keeping them secure in the safe until they are required for an evening dinner or other such occasion. I take great pride in the fact that I'm trusted to do this job. I am the only one who has the key to the safe and knows the special number combination of the lock. Therefore if anything happens to any of these expensive items it would be me that would be the first to get blamed.

Although this job would be considered dull by some standards, it suits me very well. I dislike the heat and never amble along the beach, even with a parasol. Going out to sea would be a disaster as I get terribly sick even when the waves are not at all choppy. Walking for miles around the coast or being a tour guide would just make holes in the soles of my perfectly good shoes and create blisters on my delicate feet. So sitting at this desk for most of the day, and sometimes the night, in a foyer with a cooling ceiling fan run by complicated wind-up mechanics, is a real pleasure.

I can speak six different languages in the perfect amount necessary to welcome the guests and see to their every need. This is why it came as somewhat of a surprise that I received a letter today telling me that I had been laid off work. There was no real explanation. The brief letter was neatly handwritten in fountain pen on personalised paper, signed by Flavio himself. My boss can be very considerate sometimes. When I questioned him in person, all he said was that he wants me to take an early retirement. It surely couldn't have been because of that time last week when I burst into tears because a guest found a dead cockroach in the shower. No, it could not have been that.

I knew that if I protested my sacking I wouldn't be able to get a good recommendation from him for my next job, if I was able to find one at all. Apparently however, one of the chambermaids said that someone had made a very big complaint about me. This lady had awoken at night and come down to the foyer to make a request for another blanket to be provided, as her bell wasn't working, only to see me standing in front of one of the large mirrors apparently admiring myself with some expensive jewellery around my neck that could not have belonged to me. It was of course a despicable lie. Some people just like to make trouble. They have wealth and they want power over the lives of the little people like me. This woman must have found it enjoyable to ruin my career. All because I'd told her curtly that during the summer months we put all of the extra blankets into storage in the attic, deeming them extraneous to our needs at that time of year.

I was very sad to be given my marching orders over such a slight thing. The wrong tone of voice with a little sharpness to it that appeared too unkind. And the jewellery, I was merely checking that it was in good condition and didn't need a polish. I was in no way being disrespectful to my clientele. I would never do that, particularly as I regard The Hotel Resplendent as my second home. I would miss the ruby red carpets with the gold pattern, the large ornate mirrors, and the chandelier that has sparkled over my days at reception like a thousand stars.

Then it occurred to me, rather than confront this person themself, I could get my revenge by creating a little mayhem, a little bit of chaos in the guests' carefully ordered world. If I could get them to suspect each other, or the other members of staff of causing a disruption, it would create a very difficult atmosphere for the boss.

Well, this was my plan, and I intended to execute it at night while everyone was asleep. I would need to wait until Thursday, when my late shift was due. There were to be no new arrivals that day beyond 8pm so the coast would be clear. I

67

prepared myself well. I wore underclothes that wouldn't make rustling noises while I walked. My shoes were to be flat and with soft soles so that they didn't make a noise on the ground as I walked, rather than my usual ones with the small heels whose tread echoed in the hallways. I would wear silk gloves so that no fingerprints could be found.

My aim was to create confusion and no more. So, at around 3am, I lowered the gaslights, and tiptoed along the corridors. With the master key that each member of staff possessed a copy of, I was able to quietly unlock each room, take some items and place them in somebody else's room. Not a single person stirred; I had sent a complimentary nightcap to everyone before the lights were out, with a little extra something in it to aid their slumber. The few night staff on duty had also received such a tipple and were now fast asleep slumped in their chairs, snoring away peacefully.

It took me the best part of two and a half hours to do what I had to do, rearranging things to my liking, but I was satisfied with what I had done. It wasn't as if it was a criminal offence to bamboozle the clientele. I wasn't stealing anything. But it did give me a certain thrill to think that I was being in some way disruptive to these people who are always expecting everything to be completely shipshape and in order at all times.

When the guests started to wake, I could hear small clusters of arguments breaking out between them and the staff. I went to investigate assuming the countenance of somebody completely innocent and appearing to try my utmost to help them resolve their numerous crises. I got a certain satisfaction from seeing them rattled over the mischief I had created. One elderly lady's expensive wig had been found in the lavatory of a gentleman on another floor. A young woman's private diary had found its way into the briefcase of a doctor.

A particularly fastidious man had had his smart outdoor shoes replaced by a pair of tiny ballet shoes belonging to a young prima ballerina residing on the first floor. One woman's lipsticks had been used to create a beautiful pattern on the bathroom mirror conveying a plethora of Italian swear words. I had replaced the small complimentary bottles of alcohol in the cabinet with a carton of sour milk, for one visitor who was livid he couldn't have his usual morning beverage.

When one quite well-known singer's precious little music box was found in another room where an elderly couple were staying, she was very upset, claiming they had stolen it with evil intent to deprive her of the family heirloom she'd inherited from her parents. This lady was, however, extremely gratified to get the music box back and I insisted there had been some uncanny mix up, that some cheeky elves or fairies had been creating a bit of mischief in the night. You know, she actually believed me, and the thought tickled her somewhat. She was more preoccupied in being on time for a performance later that day, and set about to get ready. The elderly couple were forgiven in such a gracious manner that it quite impressed me.

I professed to know nothing about the various guests' misplaced items. I said that if they wanted to make a complaint they must talk to the boss. He would be in at 2 o'clock, I said. But some clients were too upset to wait until then. Their day had been disrupted and that would not do. For a life neatly ordered and perfectly ship-shape, this was a disaster. Some of the guests immediately packed their bags and left. But not before creating quite a commotion. I noticed that very few of them had a sense of humour about what had happened. They had obviously got up on their high horses a long time ago and did not like being mocked or made to feel confused.

Luckily, for the remaining clients, I'd made myself extremely useful putting to rights what had gone wrong. They were so grateful, that when I told them I'd be leaving this establishment for good the following day they couldn't believe it. I was the only one that seemed to know what she was doing, they said. Without me, this hotel would be a complete shambles, they insisted. I encouraged them to let the boss know about anything they were pleased with about my conduct, as this might secure me this job for the future, and I wouldn't have to leave after all. They were only too happy to oblige. But when they appeared reluctant to return next year for their customary holiday I made the bold decision to offer them a 50% discount on their stay if booked in advance.

I had placated their querulous minds and righteous indignation, and set them back on the good, solid and secure path to being fully in control once more. They were not the only ones who were feeling in control again. When the boss heard about what had happened, he felt that I'd saved not just the day itself that was descending into chaos, with my cool-headed initiative, but also the reputation of the hotel. Not only was I to stay on, but I was to get a pay rise as well. The culprit, he would bring to justice somehow, but he knew there would be an outcry if he sacked any one of the staff on scant evidence, and he didn't want any kind of negative publicity for the hotel.

You may think it strange that I went to all this trouble to keep my job. But I had grown used to the chandelier of stars made with the light of a hundred candles, and the view onto the seafront. I was accustomed to the quiet confidence and gentle demeanour I presented in public. I liked how everyone trusted me and valued my discretion regarding all the important matters and the less important ones too. This incident was never to be spoken of again. The boss employed a new lady to work alongside me, to ease the burden of the job that hitherto had possibly been taking its toll on my wellbeing.

She is a sweet little thing, but very naïve. She stares at some of the more attractive gentlemen, and gossips about every little thing she hears. I must say that she has exceptionally good hearing. I myself pretend to be a little deaf while is she is speaking to me. I prefer not to know too much about those I serve. It helps me keep a professional distance and maintain my respect for those clients The Hotel Resplendent and all the staff value so highly. I will soon teach this good-natured young woman how to behave in a more appropriate manner as befits such a fine establishment, where everything is right and everything is proper, and yet nothing and no one is quite what they seem.

Chapter 6 – The Departure

"I thought you'd never get here." Lisa grabs my backpack from me as I step onto the boat.

"There was something I needed to do first," I say. "For a friend."

"I didn't think you had any friends except for me." Lisa looks as hurt as if I have been keeping an important secret from her.

"Just someone I met along the way," I say.

"Well, it's just the two of us now," she says, eyes sparkling fiercely.

I take a seat on the deck and ask how many days' supplies we have. "Three," she says. "That's enough for us to sail to Tunis, stopping off at Palermo on the way." I haven't eaten for a while but I don't say anything and let my stomach grumble, drowned out by the sound of the waves lapping the sides of the boat. The sea is choppy. I hope I have the strength to survive this journey without being sick. But however bad it gets, it's a lot better than travelling by plane. I have such an utter fear of flying that it's almost impossible to get me onto one unless heavily sedated.

Mum and dad used to load me up with Valium before taking me on their private jet. I'd spend the whole time slumped in the seat feeling nauseous and zombie-like. My vision was blurred and voices sounded muffled. Yet I was still too wired to sleep. They had tried hypnotherapy on me but I refused to comply, to have someone else in charge of my mind. Why they had to take me with them, I don't know. Even at 15 years old, they still treat me like a child, or their prisoner, more like. They are always bribing me with things in order not to make a scene in public that might damage their reputations. A judge and a politician certainly have a lot of allies. Their conduct and parenting skills could not and must not be brought into question. How they are regarded by others is of the utmost importance to them, and anything I feel is irrelevant to the power games they're playing.

But here, now, with Lisa, I feel a sense of relief, of the previous life I led slipping away, like the shedding of an old skin. And it is much overdue. I'd begun to develop anger issues and anorexia too. One thing they couldn't do was force me to eat. And Lord knows, they tried. And if you think it was because they cared, you're wrong. They merely wanted to tighten their controlling grip, a suffocating and demeaning grip. They claimed I was too unbalanced to make decisions of my own. Locking me in my room if I refused to temper my anger.

It was regretful to them I was a departure from the norm. They couldn't accept that I loved girls instead of boys. They tried hypnotherapy on me for that too. Needless to say, it didn't work, but only ruined any chance of us ever getting along. No love lost there, though. There never was any love to begin with.

Lisa starts up the boat and navigates out of the harbour's mouth. Amalfi recedes into the distance, the buildings look like doll's houses now, the jetty with surrounding stone boulders merges into the sea and soon all becomes a misty blur. The sun is held captive behind some grey clouds. I feel a rush of cool air whip around my body making me reach for a jumper I have at the bottom of the backpack. It's Shetland wool, grey with a white pattern; a Christmas present from Lisa. It slides over my head and onto my body like a mother's warm embrace, just not my mother's but a universal one – one that's nurturing and caring, strong, fierce, and loyal. All of that in a jumper, I hear you ask? Well, it's pretty special to me as it marked my first anniversary with Lisa.

Now it is 18 months, 2 weeks, 4 days, 13 hours, and 43 minutes since we met at midnight at a New Year's Eve party to welcome in the year of 1996. We kissed and it was a big deal at the time. It's one of the few happy memories I have and I like to relive it over and over. Seventeen more minutes have gone by and the boat is tipping to and fro as it's propelled forwards towards Palermo. I see Lisa at the wheel, focused on the journey ahead. I put my arms around her waist and rest my chin on her shoulder. She gives my short blond hair an affectionate tousle and then resumes monitoring the control panels. The boat belongs to her uncle and she has 'borrowed' it for our escape and expedition. When we reach Tunis, we will have to pretend we are sisters. No kissing or holding hands in public. I slip my hand over hers, fingers intertwined, and we grip the steering wheel together. We're on a journey into the unknown, but I feel more confident than ever before.

"You should eat something," she says. "It will give you strength. We need to reach Palermo in good health." I reluctantly release my hand from hers, peel myself away from her warm body, and descend the stairs into the cabin below. There's food in the cupboards; tins and jars and packets. The fridge is unfortunately broken. The stove, however, is not. I cook up some pasta and add a sauce and a tin of beans and some mushrooms. Perfect. I chew it carefully knowing how precious food is, knowing how lucky I am to have any at all. If there's one thing Lisa has taught me, it's how to value our resources. She doesn't come from a wealthy family as I do. She's had to make do with less of everything all of her life. She's never given me the impression she feels deprived in any way, though. I guess that must be because her parents loved her. And now we have each other and we feel like the luckiest people in the world.

I take a bowl of food up to the deck for Lisa. She tells me I need to rest. It's a long journey ahead. Back down below, I clear away the cooking equipment and move into the sleeping area. There are a double bed and a full-length mirror on the wall. I look at the reflection staring back at me. I'm gaunt and there are two dark circles under my hazel eyes. My hair looks storm-tossed. It's always sticking up in odd places so I've made a feature of it and actually emphasise its waywardness. It's streaked white from the sun and is salty from the sea. I run my fingers through it to untangle it. Odd that I am blond when my parents both have dark hair. Lisa has short hair, too. She cuts it herself and it's a decent effort. She has a long floppy fringe that sometimes obscures her eyes. But her intensity is always there, peering through the strands.

I feel sleepy. I have a lot of strength to rebuild. Three years of being undernourished have left their mark. The bed is soft and welcoming. I pull the covers over me, up to my chin, and let the gentle sway of the boat lull me off to a deep slumber. I dream of the Tunisian sun and of camel rides across the desert, of cool refreshing drinks in the shady gardens of a palace, and the shrill chirping of birds high above. Lisa is there, brown from the sun, blue eyes sparkling like the sea. And there is a young boy nearby playing with a small dog, laughing and merry, with such a great deal of love and kindness in his eyes.

I wake briefly to see a school of dolphins skimming and leaping over the waves through the porthole window, before sinking into sleep once more. No dreams this time, just a whirling sensation as if I'm on a roller coaster twisting and turning through the universe, through time itself. When I wake there is someone familiar sitting on the edge of the bed. Her face is weathered and leathery with wrinkles and her hair reaches the floor. But she has the same intense, fierce blue eyes that I know so well.

"What's happened?" I mumble and sit up in bed. My hair is long also and cascades downwards, overlapping hers. I put my hands to my face and see they are weathered, too. My face feels plumper but wrinkled also. Yet there is strength in my limbs I haven't felt in years. And speaking of years, so much time seems to have passed.

"You've been confused," says Lisa, her expression full of warmth and concern. "I've been very worried. You've been talking in your sleep."

"Who's steering the boat?" I ask anxiously.

"Karim."

"Who?"

"Our son, the one we adopted in Tunis all those years ago," says Lisa, gently.

"We have a son?" I ask, incredulously.

"You've been unwell, had a fever, we thought you wouldn't make it. It's affected your memory." Lisa takes my hands in hers, kisses me on the forehead. I see the gold ring on her finger and mine too. Wedding rings. I catch my breath. What has happened is beyond my understanding.

"Where are we going?" I ask.

"Wherever the wind may take us," is her reply.

"But I don't remember anything. I was 15, escaping on a boat with you from Amalfi, and now this."

Lisa looks serious now. "We'll help you remember all the adventures we've had until it comes back to you – until it all makes more sense."

"That may never happen," I say, feeling a little adrift in a sea of my own unfamiliar self. Past and present converge in a dizzying formation. Images spin through my mind, new and old. Lisa brings me a nourishing soup and I sip it, the tantalising exotic flavours bringing warmth to my body. Sunlight streams through the porthole window. The boat seems to have stopped in the water and is now bobbing at great speed as if the waves are quite choppy today. I see a man at the doorway, about 25 years old, tall, and lithe. Black eyes and hair and a charming grin.

"So, mother, you have emerged to greet us from the depths of your feverish slumber," he says. I feel an instant connection to him and love rises in my chest like that of a mother for her dearest child. It is automatic, a response that must have happened countless times before."

"I had to postpone my wedding," says Karim. "To be here for you. I could not rest until your fever had passed."

"Am I invited to this wedding of yours?" I ask, sheepishly.

"Invited? You organised it all, from beginning to end, every last detail is your own creation." Karim tries to flatten down his unruly hair and leans on the cabin wall, looking fully at ease with himself and the world.

"Am I a very controlling mother, then?" I ask, fearing the worst. To be so would be my worst nightmare.

"Only in the best possible sense," he replies. "You need more rest. Your mind has been tossed like the boat on the waves with this illness of yours. I will steer the ship into calmer waters." I wonder if he is still talking about my mind, the metaphorical boat, or the real boat itself, though I have to admit, nothing at the moment seems very real. Karim kisses me on the forehead and vanishes onto the upper deck. Lisa brings me some bread and an elixir of some kind that tastes bitter and medicinal. I am still trying to piece together how this all happened.

I marvel at our long tresses and the change in our appearance.

"Karim seems lovely. Well-adjusted. Kind," I tell Lisa.

"You seem surprised," she says.

"Considering my own upbringing..."

"That's long past, Devon. This is our life now."

"You stood by me all these years," I say in wonderment.

"And you, me." Lisa tilts her head as if trying to get a better understanding of me. Her expression is puzzled.

"You'll have to tell me everything," I say. "I don't want to miss a thing."

"I will, in good time. And of course, you have your journals, too. I kept them all. Thirty years of writing. You were thinking of turning them into a book. Our Tunisian adventures. You turned out to be quite a writer. I pray you still are."

The elixir is taking effect. I feel as if warm golden honey infused with sunlight is running through my veins. Lisa sees that I am relaxing.

"It is your own formula," she says. "Developed over the years, from ancient recipes. You became quite the local wise-woman with your homemade lotions and potions. I hope those memories will come back in time. There is very precious knowledge within you – within all of us." I sink back into sleep and hope that when I wake, my mind will be restored. I hear the hum of the boat's engine starting up again. And simultaneously the engine of my thoughts starts to whir. Years of memories cascade through my mind, falling into place. Is this just a dream? Is anything not? I have a sense that I am flying above it all, carried on the wind, the boat, and my loved ones, below me and distant. I am like a bird-woman flying the nest and looking for the next place to rest. My long golden hair streams out behind me, billowing in the wind like a hundred feathers. The sun beats down on my bare skin. I feel I am being beckoned to go yet higher, but I hold back. There is a strong pull from earth keeping me here. My son, my wife, they want me and need me still. I am freefalling, spiralling down in a vortex, and then I am inside my body again, on the bed, in the cabin. It is two days later when I wake. And this time there is no doubt that I am staying. The fever has passed.

We share breakfast on the deck, I, marvelling at Karim's familiarity and strangeness, and mine too, as well as Lisa's. It's a different world where a certain magic and mystery has entered in that I don't want to leave us. We are headed off to new lands and new adventures. There is a wedding to attend in Dubrovnik, Croatia – one that I have apparently organised down to the finest detail. Although a lot is still new to me, I feel oddly serene. Time has played tricks on my mind, but I trust in its unfolding. I took the road less travelled some time ago and ended up in a place that I love. I trust all is as it should be and look forward to what is ahead.

Chapter 7 – Free-Diving

My name is Eva, and I married Karim in the autumn of 2028, eight years ago. It was a small private wedding in Dubrovnik, arranged and paid for by his two mothers, bless their hearts. My own parents couldn't afford to contribute to the cost, but Karim helped out with the money he earns from his ice-cream and souvenir shop. The ice-cream he makes is divine – only from the milk of very happy cows that have a good life. He makes the concoctions himself and is now an expert at creating unlikely but delicious combinations.

The flavours he uses are unique. He makes savoury as well as sweet recipes. If you are ever on the lookout for fish-flavoured gelato, or nettle (without the sting), or curry flavour with a spicy kick to it, Karim is your man. He gives his creations inventive names, like 'Shark's Delight', 'Forest Spirit', or 'Maharaja's Surprise'. The children, especially, love his ideas. It's nice to see them enjoying the icy cold treats, particularly as we don't have any children of our own.

I have rheumatoid arthritis but this doesn't seem to worry Karim. It takes a special kind of person to take on board someone like me whose condition may deteriorate in time. But Karim has the power to see beyond my limitations. In fact, for the wedding, he decorated my wheelchair beautifully, according to his own designs. Instead of trying to conceal this cumbersome object, he made a feature of it and spray-painted all the metalwork gold before covering it in garlands of fresh roses. That was truly a day to remember but to be honest we try to live every day as if it is a celebration of life. We never know when it might be our last together. People can often focus on my disability. Some of them pity me because I use a wheelchair. Perhaps they wonder how I manage to turn it this way and that with ease over the narrow cobbled streets or what it is like to be unable to walk.

Little do they know that when I'm in the sea, I become somebody else, almost a fish, an aquiline free-diver with special abilities at holding my breath. I have been able to do this since I was a child. My father taught me. He used to dive for pearls but I have been diving for years and have not found even one. However, the island where we live is said to be one of the pearls of the Adriatic, and so I spend my entire time living upon a very beautiful jewel. The forests are indeed like emeralds, the sunlight like gold, and the mountains like silver. The sea, of course, is a jewel of Sapphire blue.

And anyway, as my grandmother used to say, it's pearls of wisdom that are the most important, as long as you don't throw them before swine. She kept pigs on her small farm and perhaps she lost a pearl earring there one day and it was trampled underfoot by one of the pregnant sows and mangled in the mud. She always said she'd lost a valuable family heirloom when she was young. Perhaps that's what it was.

My grandmother always wears black. No matter how hot or cold it is or for what occasion she is required to be present, it's always long black dress and a black headscarf that she chooses. Her white hair peeps through and her green eyes sparkle with the wisdom of 80 years spent on this earth. She is no fool even though she can't read. I tried to teach her but she wasn't interested. She knows about the land and how to cultivate the earth for a fruitful harvest and how to cook hearty meals for her family with all the ingredients that she grows on the farm. And that's not all she knows how to do.

She was at the wedding, sitting in the shade of an olive tree, cooling herself with a fan made of fabric and wood. She makes a lot of things from the hemp she grows. She made my baby shoes and also several rugs for the house. All the yarn was spun on a traditional spinning wheel and woven on her handmade loom. She crochets and knits like it's a religion. I remember how focused she is at such times, that I can't break her concentration whatever I do.

She was even crocheting at the wedding; a cardigan for the winter for Karim. She is fond of him, their communication is beyond words as they can't understand each other's language. They both love me, and love is the most universal language of all. She makes things for our souvenir shop; shell necklaces and wall-hangings and crocheted shawls embellished with beads. We take no profit for ourselves from those items of hers, which are very popular with the tourists. We even have her picture in the window. Like our marriage, our little shop is eight years old. As with any relationship, there are times when things can become a bit strained. My health is slowly worsening and I've noticed Karim being more protective of me, overprotective, some might argue. We just need time apart occasionally, and that is the role that my free-diving plays, though this is getting harder as I tire more easily than before.

We are allowed to have our own friends, Karim and I, without the other one necessarily having to be a part of it. We both like this arrangement. But sometimes I notice he acts a bit jealous when I go out for an evening with my ladies, leaving him behind. I ask if he wants to accompany me but he acts aloof and distant and says he is entitled to a bit of peace away from laughing and giggling women. I think he feels we may be making fun of him, and although it happened on only one occasion I can recall, that has coloured the rest of his thinking regarding our social activities together.

Today Karim and I are going further down the coast. He says he has a surprise for me at the home of an acquaintance of his. I'm excited as it's not often I get a surprise like this, but I think it's Karim who is the most excited of all. He drives carefully and steadily, eyes firmly fixed on the road. Every now and then he says: "I know you'll love it, just wait and see." I nod in agreement, not knowing what to expect.

We pull into the driveway of a large house with another building attached, like a large barn, but in this case, it's a workshop. The door is open and I can see all sorts of machinery on the inside and a man in overalls facing away from us until he turns and waves and I realise it's actually a woman.

We are greeted warmly and offered Turkish coffee, which I accept graciously. There is a large object covered in a blanket nearby. I guess this is to be the gift I am to be offered and there will soon be a big reveal. I am curious as to what it is. I guess that it's some kind of washing machine for the wheelchair. It tends to get very grubby when we go into the forest or over the muddy path down to the river.

Or perhaps it's something else; a miniature distillery to make our own cider. We certainly have a bumper crop of apples every year from our orchard. I sip my coffee patiently while Karim and this woman who I learn is called Branka, finalise some details on paper. They are so absorbed in what they're doing that I leave them to it and navigate my old clumsy wheelchair around the workshop. It's full of every conceivable kind of contraption. Numerous old conventional items have been taken apart and remade into something new.

There are the bare skeletons of washing machines and cars, motorbikes, and food processors, their parts having been salvaged for some other purpose, no doubt. The workshop smells of rubber and petrol and rust, but I must admit that this place is exciting, full of possibilities where old and unwanted gadgets and appliances are repurposed and given a second life. I wonder if

Branka has built me a robot exoskeleton to help me get around more easily, but I cannot see our small seaside town adapting to the sight of such a contraption. I am beckoned over by Karim.

"Do you like my little Palace of Invention?" asks Branka, proudly.

"I do, though it's unusual to find a woman at the helm of so much mechanical equipment," I say.

"My father was an engineer," she says by way of explanation. "These creations of mine are my babies."

Branka walks over to the covered apparatus and with a great theatrical flourish, as if she is a magician, removes the cloth and lets it drop to the floor to reveal a strange and wonderful sight.

As far as I can tell, it's a wheelchair of some kind, only a very futuristic one. There is a roof on the top above where my head would be, covered in solar panels. Below, the seat itself is covered in a waterproof turquoise fabric that mimics velvet.

The seat is padded like an armchair, but slim and sleek. There are no wheels, but instead a ring of rubber around the base. And then I see the most remarkable thing of all: it is hovering six inches off the ground.

The hand controls look as if they've been borrowed from an old gaming console and the armrests have an air about them of Italian furniture design from the 1960s. Under the seat is a compartment for stowing away shopping or whatever else I want to take with me.

"It does 30 kilometres an hour," says Branka. "And can hover up to 20 metres in the air." I gasp.

"Not only that," she says, "It can travel smoothly over any surface at ground level and skim across water too. It's solar powered and can run for 60 hours of use on one four-hour charge. And on top of all that, you'll never have to worry about stairs again."

"Who's paying for all of this?" I ask, fearing that we will be in debt for years to come paying off the cost.

"It's yours for free as it's my prototype. If it's a success, I will have more manufactured, the sale of which will cover the initial cost of developing my idea." Branka turns the chair around so I can see the back of it. It's studded with pearls that spell my name and something more: 'Eva Forever', it says.

"That's your husband's idea," says Branka. Karim smiles.

"Can I try it out?" I ask.

"For sure," says Branka, as she presses a button and the contraption descends to ground level. I ease myself out of the old wheelchair and into the new one. Only it isn't exactly a wheelchair anymore, but a hovercraft with a lot of style. I wonder what my grandmother would think of this. I strap myself in as if I'm about to embark on the world's first mission to the moon. Branka places a metallic purple biker's helmet over my head and straps it on.

"Are you sure this is safe?" I ask Karim and Branka both. They nod their heads in a serious fashion. I suppose they must have tested it dozens of times. I'm given brief instructions on how the controls work. Branka hands me the key and I turn on the ignition. A gentle hum emanates from the machine like the purring of a cat.

I press a green button. The machine lifts two feet into the air. It's lucky that the barn has such a high roof because that's where I'm headed. They are shouting from below and waving their arms but I don't hear them. I am straight out of the open skylight and ascending fast. I turn and twist and do somersaults, all while strapped into the chair. I am in a sky-ballet. Free-diving above the land as opposed to in the sea.

I press another button and I make a smooth descent onto the lawn, closely missing the car. Karim runs to my side, a look of concern on his face. But then he breaks into a smile of delight and wonder. "It's beyond my expectations," he says. "Now you'll have all the freedom you deserve."

Branka seems happy with the flying skills I have demonstrated.

"It's a shame you couldn't have made a two-seater one, so Karim can tag along" I say jokingly.

"I'm working on a second vehicle that can attach to this one, so husband and wife can both travel in style." Branka goes inside and brings out some sketches so I can see what she is working on.

"I prefer it as it is," I say. "After all, it's about getting some independence back, isn't it?" Karim reluctantly agrees.

Branka shrugs her shoulders, screws up her sketches in her fist, and tosses them behind her on the ground.

"Honey, I'm not sure you should be going out on your own in this thing, unsupervised," Karim says.

"I thought that was the point," I say. "Not to havc to rely on you so much."

"You have to let her make her own decisions," says Branka. It's odd because that's what my grandmother often says to him too. I notice also that Branka has the same intense green eyes of my grandmother, and the white, flawless complexion. If I believed in such things as time-travel, I would've sworn that she was a younger version of my relative somehow transported here, now.

I remember a story from my childhood when grandmother told me she was related to Nikola Tesla. This would explain why she understood machines very well, even mending my father's car on a few occasions. It was like her sixth sense, totally untaught but from a place deep inside her. Branka and I exchange farewells. She doesn't seem to recognise me except as the wife of Karim that she has only just met. She is abrupt, even in the brevity of her smile. Like all great inventors, she has things to do. One project ends and another begins. Thoughts of my grandmother begin to fade away.

"I don't want the old wheelchair back," I say to Karim, once we are alone.

"We'll leave it behind," he says. "I'm sure Branka can use the old parts for something. This is a fresh start." He opens the passenger seat door for me like the gentleman he is. I'm lucky I'm still mobile enough to transfer from the hover-chair to the car seat myself.

The various parts of the old wheelchair will be reused and made into something. I settle into the passenger seat and Karim loads the hovercraft into the back. Luckily the roof of the contraption can fold down to fit smaller spaces. I feel energised by today's outing. Karim is pleased to see some of my vigour return. I thank him for his gift.

"That is not all," he says. "I can make you an ice-cream when we get home. A brand new recipe just for you."

"What'll it have in it?" I ask.

"Something that has fire and boldness," he says. "I have just the thing. I'll call it Jalapeno Jive."

He turns the radio on. As one tune ends and an ancient ballad called 'Dancing Through Time' starts to play. Now that really would be something else, if Branka had invented a time machine too.

I look over at Karim and I know that look. He wants to talk about something serious. He is formulating his words carefully, silently, before he begins to talk.

"My friend Marko's sister went to Medjugorje and was cured of her chronic back pain. Her operation was cancelled." Karim stares straight ahead. He knows I don't like the topic of cures and quick-fix solutions, least of all religious ones.

"I don't believe in the power of the Blessed Virgin Mary," I say. "Those kids that saw the visions, they could've been high on drugs."

Karim inhales deeply and then tells me his unexpected news.

"I have two coach tickets to get us there, and for the connecting boat trip. The hotel too."

I stare at him in disbelief.

"What about our shop? Who will run that? We can't afford to lose income," I say, cross that he hasn't consulted me on this.

"Your grandmother said she would run the shop for a few days with a friend of hers who can read and do math." Karim's voice is steady and strong, unwavering like his determination.

So, it's all sorted and I have no say in the matter. The rest of the journey home we are in silence. I wonder if getting the gift of the new mode of transport was just to soften me up to go on this pointless expedition. Virgin Mary, indeed! I would be better off praying to Poseidon. I decide not to make a fuss. If this is what will keep Karim happy, I will do it for him. I just hope he will be able to cope with the disappointment when I leave Medjugorje without a cure. Nothing short of a miracle would change his mind about going and I lost faith in them a long time ago.

But as I think more about it, my indignation lessens. Karim must want me to have my independence back too or he would not be seeking some kind of a cure for me, however irrational it might seem. I vow to put more effort into my physiotherapy, which basically involves swimming for an hour a day. I try to imagine what life would be like with more mobility, more energy. Perhaps we could expand our small souvenir and ice-cream shop into a restaurant. My grandmother's traditional recipes would be popular with tourists and locals. If we make some profit, Karim could buy our own small boat that he's always dreamed of and we could have holidays at sea, travelling from island to island.

I go to bed in a more positive mood, believing that my health's deterioration is not in fact inevitable. I will go to Medjugorje with an open mind and leave my cynical attitude behind. Scepticism might get in the way of any healing if there is any healing to be had. I look at Karim sleeping, his long eyelashes like tiny black feathers. I wonder what he dreams about, if even while asleep he is concerned for me. His arm reaches around my waist and pulls me close.

Whatever happens we'll get through this as a team. I roll towards him and put my arm around his waist. He stirs briefly then falls back into slumber.

"I love you," I whisper. "And I know you love me, though I make it hard for you sometimes with my angry moods." But then I remember that a worthless, rough piece of grit is transformed into a smooth pearl if you are lucky. *Let all the rough places in my heart become like pearls, smoothed and covered by understanding and compassion,* I think to myself, and realise it's a kind of prayer. I have not prayed since I was a child, since I first got ill. Well, now is as good a time as any to begin again. I feel a small tight place of anger in my chest soften and melt away as I sink into sleep. I dream about a restaurant that is open to the night sky, resplendent with stars. Two people are dancing there beneath the moonlight, but I can only see their silhouettes and shadows, merged as one entity, moving to the sweet music of time.

Chapter 8 – Chicken and Banana Supreme

My name is Anna, and I'm Eva's grandmother. Perhaps she has told you a bit about me already? I hope so. I think I've had quite an influence on her life. I told her to keep going when she felt like quitting because the pain was too much. I told her that good things will happen in the future if she's patient. Then Karim crossed her path and her life was never the same again. Destiny brought them together and it's destiny that can also tear them apart if they're not careful. But Fate isn't written in stone. Today's actions determine the future.

This morning I'm looking after the ice-cream shop. We're running out of Pizza Perfect and Olive and Apple. They seem to be popular flavours. Karim has shown me how the ice-cream maker works and I remember all the instructions. I intend to make a concoction or two of my own. Chicken and banana will make the perfect couple; main course and dessert all in one gelato. Then I can whip up an apricot and meringue medley with some grated cheese on the top.

Behind the ice-cream counter is the rest of the shop, selling souvenirs, some of which I've made. Karim collects shells on the beach when he goes for his morning run, and I crochet them into shawls and summer hats, belts and scarves. I am now so quick with my fingers that I can complete one item in an afternoon. The children say my hands are full of magic. My cat thinks so too. She loves to be held in my hands and stroked. All the neighbourhood strays are jealous of the attention she gets. They hang around the door hoping for some human contact. I leave food and water out for them and get medicines for them if they are sick.

Today, two of them have followed me to the shop and are basking in the sun outside. This encourages the children, who kneel down and stroke them, whispering sweet words into their ears. The cats are very gentle with them, even when the children pull their tails for fun or rub their fur the wrong way.

I'm sitting in the shade indoors, knitting, while my friend Maria dishes out the ice-cream. Across the street is an artist making portraits of passers-by. There aren't any cars or bicycles here as most of the old town is for pedestrians alone. The lanes of shops are narrow, with cobbled paving, centuries old. The tourists love this place, but the locals too can be seen at the small supermarket, buying freshly baked bread, or going to the hairdressers next door. I've not cut my hair in 17 years, since my dear husband died. When it's unravelled at night, it reaches to my knees. I like having something to keep them warm when I curl up in bed at night. Evenings here can be very cool, even in summer.

Marko owns the supermarket opposite. He is about my age and has a wonderful moustache, silver and jaunty. He likes to visit our shop to buy ice-cream and say hello. He wants to try every flavour. I want to tell him that the ice-cream often gets caught in his moustache but I don't want to be rude. He's interested in my craft handiwork. As a young man he made fishing nets. He wants me to mend some that his nephews, who are fishermen, need fixing. I agree. The pay is good. A lot depends on those nets. Marko has also promised me some copper thread if I can complete the task quickly. He is offered all sorts of things by customers in exchange for the groceries at his shop, so has surplus to spare.

The nephews who are in their early 20's are chatty and warm, sun-kissed and scrawny. One of them whistles a lot and the other one sings. I ask Maria to give them free ice-cream as I mend their nets. It keeps them quiet for a while. After the job is done and they have been out fishing again, they bring me a very large fish for my supper. I put it in the freezer with the gelato to keep it fresh until the end of the day so as not to attract the cats. Marko brings me the copper thread. He's pleased with the work I've done for his relatives, whose livelihoods depend on fishing.

Copper is known for its healing properties. It can help with aches and pains and arthritis. The first thing I do is knit Eva some gloves and some knee-high socks. The copper is very malleable and not at all sharp. I knit it together with turquoise silk yarn for added protection. Silk is believed to prevent dark forces from penetrating someone's aura. I learnt this from Maria who is somewhat psychic and interested in the healing arts, though not psychic enough to win the lottery, unfortunately. She reads the tealeaves for people in exchange for bread and fruit and wine. She won't accept money. She says that would cheapen the whole enterprise and she wants to keep it classy.

Maria wears French perfume and Italian scarves. She has her admirers that keep coming back. Some say it isn't only reading of tealeaves that she offers her clients but these are just rumours. People like to gossip because they have nothing better to do and it makes them feel important to put others down. I block my ears to it and secretly despise those who like to create a rumour, particularly if it's about a good friend of mine.

The next day I knit more items with the copper. No matter how much I use, the original amount doesn't appear to diminish. I'm able to knit at triple the speed and my hands don't ache as they usually do. Towards the end of the day I've completed two cloaks of tightly crocheted copper and silk yarn. They shimmer in the sun as I display them outside on two chairs. The stray cats have gone and Maria will soon close up the shop. Just as I'm about to bring the cloaks back in, two sisters emerge from out of the supermarket and cross the pebbled street to where I stand.

They seem transfixed by the colours of the copper garments and ask to try them on. They chatter excitedly to one another, admiring their reflections in the shop window opposite. Their swaying movements bring the cloaks alive so that they sparkle and shimmer like sunlight on the sea. They might be mermaids, or they might be fairies, it's hard to tell. They offer me twice what the garments are worth and I graciously accept. It is a compliment to be offered such an amount.

I wish them a good evening and as I lean forward to receive the money, I notice one of the women has one green eye and one blue, like the wolf I saw in my childhood preying on the chicken coup. My father shot her in the heart with a shotgun fired from a distance. He said he misfired the gun and only intended to sound a warning shot at the she-wolf and not kill her. The image flashes into my mind and I'm startled. For an instant, I see the wolf's face superimposed upon the young woman's and then it fades. The same eyes look back at me with warmth and wisdom but it's the woman who possesses them now. Years later, father told me it wasn't the chickens the wolf was after but me. He had not in fact misfired the gun. It was a story he made up to make me less afraid.

After cooking up the entrails in a stew to feed his children, father had turned the wolf-skin into mittens for us. The bones were crushed and used to nourish the soil and the head was mounted on the wall above the fireplace. But it was hollow so that when father went into the forest to fetch water he wore it as a hat to ward off attacks from other wolves. Every full moon he would go outside and howl at the white sphere in the sky, and in the distance, wolves would howl back. They never visited the farm again but always kept a respectful distance.

Tomorrow I will make a copper dress and a copper jacket with red yarn from the wool of my neighbour's goats that I have spun into skeins. Perhaps for a husband and wife. Thinking of this, I remember Karim and Eva and their trip to Medjugorje. Before we close up the shop, I ask Maria to read the tealeaves left over from my afternoon brew. We sit down at a small table inside and she turns over the cup in the saucer and rotates it three times, and studies the remains of the leaves with great concentration, her brow furrowed like the earth. For a moment I hold my breath, expecting some bad news. Perhaps this wolf-like woman's appearance at the shop was a bad omen. The money in my pocket that I earned from the cloaks, however, tells me otherwise.

Maria sucks in the air sharply, and then lets it out in a rush. I feel her warm, fragrant breath on my face, smelling of oranges and cinnamon. There has been an unexpected incident with Karim and Eva and they are heading home early. This is all she will say. For once, I wish she wouldn't be so confidential. Eva is my family after all. But no, all she will say is that they will arrive tomorrow on the afternoon boat and that things have changed between them. She is being so mysterious, but I will have to be patient and await their return to find out more.

*

Karim and I spent the first night at the hotel hardly speaking. "Eva, Eva, talk to me," he said, pleading with me, but I was silent. I'd felt seasick on the boat journey over to the mainland and the coach ride to Medjugorje twisted and turned around many potentially lethal bends in the road, with a sheer drop on one side that a car had tumbled over the week before, killing all the passengers. I was feeling very edgy. Plus, I was concerned about the hover-chair in the luggage compartment on the side of the vehicle crashing about and getting damaged by heavy suitcases. I needn't have worried. There wasn't a scratch on it when we arrived. Well, that is one miracle already, I thought to myself.

We had to leave the hover-chair outside the tiny hotel and Karim had to carry me up the stairs to our room. Why hadn't he booked ground floor accommodation? All of those rooms were already booked, he said. I think he just wanted to carry me over the threshold and into the bedroom like he did when we were first married. He asked me why I wasn't wearing my wedding ring. I had put on some weight, I said. It no longer fitted.

I'll admit I have been eating more lately. I have a new energy, a nervous kind of liveliness I hadn't had before and the tiredness is less. It's almost as if the arthritis is in remission. I'm not sure what Karim is trying to achieve or prove by bringing me here to this supposedly sacred site. The thought of my health deteriorating worries him, but it's only a thought, I tell him, think about something else. People have claimed to receive healing here and to find a greater peace inside. I don't want a greater peace inside, I had too much of that while feeling tired before now. That was an enforced peace I didn't like at all with frustration buried deep within it.

On the morning of the first day there, we're offered only one choice and unfortunately I never did like scrambled eggs. Karim is worried that I leave the plate half-full. Five days of this and I'll be able to wear my wedding ring again, if I can find it. The last time I remember having it on was when I was doing the washing up at our shop beside the ice-cream maker, and I'd taken it off and put it on the window ledge, but then somehow it vanished and what with everything else going on, I'd forgotten to search for it.

Karim manages to scrounge some fruit and yoghurt from the hotel owner for me and I'm grateful because I feel starving hungry. He really is trying his best to be so considerate, despite my irritability, that I know why I fell in love with him in the first place. We're in walking distance of the sacred site and my hover-chair amply skips along, an inch off the ground beside my husband.

When we reach a place known as Apparition Hill, I see pilgrims climbing up it in great numbers. The path ascending is rocky and steep so I decide to change gears in my machine, that I have named Pegasus. I rise twenty feet off the ground and hover to the top of the hill, slowly and steadily. I'm startled to see people fall to their knees and make the sign of the cross and assume a supplicating prayer position below me as I pass by.

Perhaps it's my shoulder-length wavy brown hair, alabaster skin and green eyes combined with the simple blue linen dress and white scarf I'm wearing, but I swear they think I'm the Virgin Mary. I shake my head and say, "No, you are all mistaken." Many in the crowd respond by calling out "Please forgive me my sins." One even cries, "My angel, you are here at last!" Angel? I think. Do I have such an androgynous appearance? Meanwhile Karim is looking embarrassed that I should be mistaken for a holy being.

"Come down from there," he cries.

"How dare you say that to the Virgin Mary," chastises one of the believers.

"That's my wife," he says.

"You mean to say you're Joseph?" comes the reply.

As I descend from the sky, an exasperated Karim meets me at the top of the hill. People close in and want to touch me. One even pulls my scarf away and buries it in her bag. Karim is being as protective as he can, trying to keep them away and stop their hands from touching my body.

"I think we'd better leave," he says.

"We only just got here," I say with a smile, as I press a lever and fly into the air once more to gasps from the crowd.

Back at the hotel I'm looking pale and feeling shaky. Karim insists on calling the local doctor. After a brief examination in private, he assures me I'm okay but need to take some iron tablets and rest. Karim thinks the stress of visiting this holy place has proved too much for me. He doesn't want this morning's fiasco to be repeated and insists we return home.

He's suddenly in good spirits that I've perked up after hearing we'll be leaving, and the good feeling between us lasts until we arrive back at the harbour's mouth of our lovely old town by the sea. Karim refuses to allow me to use my hover-chair to ascend more than 3 inches off the ground, in case I have a fall. He seems to think I'm less competent and more fragile now I'm a paler version of myself, so to speak. At first I feel cross but I let it pass. I think he's right. I need to be especially careful now.

Grandmother is waiting for us when we get home, with a delicious deep-fried dough dish she had made. Each succulent shape is sprinkled with sugar. As a child I liked to find the meaning in each shape; sometimes a duck, or a monkey. Today mine is in the shape of a swan.

When Karim is out of the room, Grandmother hands me a crocheted necklace of copper with my wedding ring attached as a pendent.

"Where did you find it?" I ask incredulously. I had looked everywhere for it.

"In the strawberry and peppermint gelato, courtesy of Marko's grandson who lost his wobbly front tooth in the place of his fortunate discovery," she says.

I tell my grandmother the news I have known for some time, that I am pregnant with twins. She gasps with joy and her eyes moisten until a tear falls onto her cheek. She embraces me in her warm plump arms that smell of sun and sea and earth. More tears fall, as do her sweet reassuring words into my ear. She quickly fetches a blanket to cover my legs and abdomen and keep me warm. When Karim comes back into the room my grandmother winks at me and discreetly leaves us alone together. He has brought me a beer, thinking it will give me strength.

"No," I say, patting my stomach.

"But you're not that fat," he says. "It will give you strength."

"It isn't good for the babies," I say.

"The babies?" he says in disbelief.

"Twins," I say. "Two girls."

"You're certain?"

"Completely."

He drops to the ground and embraces me, resting his head on my stomach and crying happy tears.

"We have our miracle," he says. I insist on making it clear that the miracle occurred several weeks before our visit to the scared site and not because of it.

One day, our children will be running through the streets barefoot and healthy, playing with the other children and eating scoopfuls of tasty ice-cream of every flavour imaginable. I hold onto the wedding ring as if it's a magical amulet of some kind. With the other hand I enfold Karim's hand in mine just as we did on our wedding day. It is dark outside now. I see a shooting star across the sky leaving a trail of light. I hope it is a portentous sign. Wherever through time and space our twin girls travel I hope they will unravel their own wonderful tales.

Chapter 9 – An Ending

I pull the cloak more tightly around me. In the forest it's cool and the canopy blocks out much of the sun's warmth. My sister Zlata has gone on ahead and I've stayed behind, picking the sweet strawberries that grow beside the path and a little beyond. It is a windless day and nothing stirs except for the beating of my heart within my chest. The copper of the cloak shimmers under the dappled light. I look up and see the mass of interlocking branches and leaves silhouetted against the grey sky. Underfoot the crisp twigs snap as I pass and the soles of my shoes hit the pebbles and small stones in a rhythm like a drumbeat.

There was a time when I didn't ever want my twin sister to leave me behind, but now I relish these times alone, especially in the forest. I drink in the aroma of wet earth and moss, leaf litter and tree bark, woody and rich. I sometimes go in search of the trees' amber resin containing fossilized plants and insects, but not today. Today I have to be mindful of the mother bear that has been sighted in the local village several times this month. One swipe of the bear's claws across the jugular and I'd be dead.

When I was three, father brought a bear cub into the house. I cried tears of fury because I new this meant someone had killed its mother. The cub's fur was coarse and its black eyes gleamed. Father fed it goat's milk and honey. The latter was an expensive delicacy we could ill afford to spare. He built the creature a pen behind the house, and hand-reared it until it was almost grown. The villagers came to see the spectacle of the bear splashing in a wooden tub father had built for it. He taught it some tricks and kept it tethered to the front porch at night to scare away the wolves. But the bear just slept and wasn't a very good guard. Then one day, father woke to find the bear had gone – it had ripped out its tether and disappeared deep into the protection of the dark forest, he presumed.

I suspect that the bear turning up at the village looking for food is father's bear. She doesn't fear humans, foolish creature, and one day she will be shot dead if she's not careful. In the air is a faint mist. I almost don't see the mushrooms concealed behind leaves at the foot of a tree. They are edible ones. I take my knife and sever some of them from their roots. But all the while I have a sense I am being watched. Then I hear it, the distant gunshot. It echoes around me but there are more mushrooms to collect. I crouch low again and select the largest ones, leaving the little ones to grow some more before they're harvested.

Then I feel the warm breath on my neck and the snout nuzzling my ear. I hold myself still and try not to move, but I have to breathe. I make my breaths long and slow and the forest mist seems to be coming out of me now and swirling around, weaving some enchantment. I turn slowly to see two small bear cubs walking away and the mother bear rearing up on her hind legs and sniffing the air. She drops down suddenly and charges at me. I tell her to stop, and flick my wrist and snap my fingers as father once did to get his bear to lie down, but this she-bear is not responding. She closes in, coming within several inches of me and I step back, pressed up against the tree.

I shield my head with my arms, hoping the blow of her razor-clawed paw won't be fatal. Terrified, I'm trying to keep as still as I can so as not to provoke her, but inside I'm trembling. The fear rises like a cold liquid in my veins and nerves. I prepare myself to die. I take a deep breath, thinking it will be my last, but then a gnarling, snarling mass of teeth and white and grey fur, descends from the tree and sinks its fangs into the mother bear's shoulder. The bear cries out in pain and as I step out of the way, she swipes the wolf from her body. It hits the ground but, angrier now, it leaps at the bear's neck, gashing a deep wound that drips berry red liquid onto the earth. I breathe fast now, relieved at my fortunate escape. I slowly calm down, and the liquid coldness inside my body turns to honey warmth once more.

In the distance, the cubs cry out and the mother bear turns and lumbers after them on all fours, limping. The wolf lies exhausted at my feet, breathing rapidly. I look into her eyes, one green and one brown like mine. She has a gash several inches long across her chest, oozing blood. She has been so heroic, selfless, even. I don't know why she wanted to save me but now I feel like we are kin, bonded by this one event.

"There, there, little wolf," I say, thinking that one life-saving favour deserves another. I wrap her in my copper cloak and carry her over my shoulders to the hut in the forest where my sister and I live. My sibling is not home yet and so I lay the wolf in her warm bed, the cloak still wrapped around her. I light the fire, tossing in the firewood in generous measure. The wolf shivers.

She has ribs showing and can't have eaten for some time. I get some dried meat from the kitchen stores and steep it in boiling water before feeding the slivers to the hungry animal. She tries to lick her wound. I make a poultice of herbs and apply it, wrapping it to her body with bandages.

As she sleeps, I watch over her in my rocking chair, the one my grandfather made for my mother when she was pregnant with me. He was a furniture maker. Each room boasts the outcome of many years of skilful labour, from cabinets with hidden drawers in pinewood to wardrobes in the Austrian style made of walnut. They all lend a certain austere elegance to our dwelling place. Zlata and I are neither austere nor elegant. Zlata is the earthy one who milks the goats and tends to our allotment. I am the one who knows about medicines from herbs and how to cook delicious meals (so she tells me) from a variety of simple home grown produce.

I hear a gentle tread on the porch. It's my sister returned with a small basket of berries and an enamel jug of fresh goat's milk.

"I rushed home. I sensed something was wrong," she says before spotting the she-wolf in her bed.

"You've rescued another helpless creature, sister. When will you learn we cannot afford all your acts of charity." She wipes her brow with the back of her hand and crouches at the side of the bed to take a closer look at our new acquisition.

"This one's different," I say. "She saved my life. I was obligated to save hers too."

"I see," says Zlata raising the cloak to look at the wolf's body.

"I think you saved more than one life, here," she tells me, pointing to the distended belly of the wolf that I thought may have been a result of malnutrition or worms. Zlata feels the abdomen and confirms the wolf is soon to have a litter of pups. This is more than I bargained for.

"I draw the line at a wolf giving birth in my bed." Zlata leaves the house and returns with a bundle of dry hay that she lays near the fire. This is going to be a long night.

We take turns staying awake and keeping vigil, both for the wolf's time of readiness to give birth and also the reappearance of the mother bear. I have father's shotgun beside me, just in case. We have moved the wolf to the bed of hay. She is very quiet but stirs occasionally and watches me with her eyes of different colours. I feel more connected to her now, like she is the harbinger of some important news.

Why she saved my life, I still don't know. Perhaps in some other time and place we were bonded too. Perhaps she remembers and knows me well. I remove the poultice to apply a fresh supply of herbs to the wound but to my surprise there is almost no trace of the injury now. My medicinal concoctions have never worked this quickly before. It must be the effects of the healing copper in the cloak, or some enchantment I'm not aware of, woven into the deep knowledge of the forest, bestowed upon us for showing mercy to each other.

Zlata wakes suddenly. She tells me she's had a dream that the wolf's pups are imminent. We peel back the cloak wrapped around our charge and wait expectantly. Then one by one, they emerge from the dreaming wolf; seven stories – not wolves at all – written in light on the wings of birds that then dissolve as if made of smoke. These tales from her deepest thoughts have pictures too, made of light but transparent like water and as ephemeral as a butterfly in flight. This deftly woven tapestry of words and images of light that emerge are secrets we must keep for the future so we can't tell them to anyone. Once the stories have emerged, and we have totally absorbed them into our very being, the wolf dissolves into mist as if she herself had been a dream. We sit in silence, the place where all things begin and end. We wrap the copper cloaks around us, eat the berries and then disappear into the forest once more. No bears trouble us. And the mist has lifted to reveal a dark blue sky beyond the canopy, covered in a million stars. Each star is a dream and each dream is a story, waiting to fall into the mind of someone fast asleep.